Celebrations

Happy Valentine's Day!

Elizabeth Ritter

PowerKiDS press.

New York

Published in 2017 by The Rosen Publishing Group, Inc.
29 East 21st Street, New York, NY 10010

First Edition

Managing Editor: Nathalie Beullens-Maoui
Editor: Melissa Raé Shofner
Book Design: Michael Flynn
Illustrator: Continuum Content Solutions

Cataloging-in-Publication Data

Names: Ritter, Elizabeth.
Title: Happy Valentine's Day! / Elizabeth Ritter.
Description: New York : PowerKids Press, 2017. | Series: Celebrations | Includes index.
Identifiers: ISBN 9781499426731 (pbk.) | ISBN 9781499429473 (library bound) | ISBN 9781499426748 (6 pack)
Subjects: LCSH: Valentine's Day–Juvenile literature.
Classification: LCC GT4925.R57 2017 | DDC 394.2618–dc23

Manufactured in the United States of America

CPSIA Compliance Information: Batch #BW17PK: For Further Information contact Rosen Publishing, New York, New York at 1-800-237-9932

Contents

Su	Mo	Tu	We	Th	Fr	Sa
			1	2	3	4
5	6	7	8	9	10	11
12	13	(14)	15	16	17	18
19	20	21	22	23	24	25
26	27	28				

Tomorrow is Valentine's Day.
We will celebrate at school.

My dad helps make cards for my class.

We use colored paper,
markers, and glue.

I make a special card for Miss Jones.

It's purple and has lots of glitter.

9

My mom bakes strawberry cupcakes.

I help her
decorate them.
Yum!

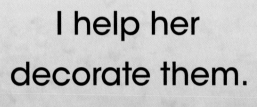

At school the next day, we get a surprise.

Miss Jones hung up hearts!

We can't wait to hand out
our valentines.

I get eight cards
from my friends.

15

At snack time, I share the cupcakes. Emily gives everyone a piece of chocolate.

Then we sit in a circle on the rug.

Miss Jones reads us a story about friendship.

We even learn a special
Valentine's Day song.

Everyone claps and sings.

Sending lots of love your way.
Have a Happy Valentine's Day!

Words to Know

cupcakes

glue

Index

24

OCT 0 2 2017

■SCHOLASTIC
News
Nonfiction Readers

A Peachick Grows Up

by Katie Marsico

Children's Press®
A Division of Scholastic Inc.
New York Toronto London Auckland Sydney
Mexico City New Delhi Hong Kong
Danbury, Connecticut

These content vocabulary word builders are for grades 1–2.

Subject Consultant: Susan H. Gray, MS, Zoology

Reading Consultant: Cecilia Minden-Cupp, PhD, Former Director of the Language and Literacy Program, Harvard Graduate School of Education, Cambridge, Massachusetts

Photographs © 2007: Alamy Images/Juniors Bildarchiv: cover background, 23 bottom left; Animals Animals/ Miriam Agron: 19; Corbis Images: 5 top right, 10 (Robert Pickett), 23 top right (Kevin Schafer), back cover, 1, 5 bottom left, 7 (Christof Wermter/zefa); Getty Images: 2, 20 top right, 21 top left (Digital Zoo/Digital Vision), 13 (Dorling Kindersley), 4 bottom right, 6 (Cyril Laubscher/Dorling Kindersley); Minden Pictures/Norbert Wu: 23 bottom right; Nature Picture Library Ltd./Reinhard/Arco: 23 top left; NHPA: front cover insets, 4 top, 4 bottom left, 5 top left, 12, 17, 20 bottom right, 20 center left, 21 center right (Joe Blossom), 15, 21 bottom (Khalid Ghani); Nolte Stock Photo/Minerva Nolte: 5 bottom right, 9, 11, 20 top left.

Book Design: Simonsays Design!
Book Production: The Design Lab

Library of Congress Cataloging-in-Publication Data
Marsico, Katie, 1980–
   A peachick grows up / by Katie Marsico.
       p. cm. — (Scholastic news nonfiction readers)
   Includes bibliographical references.
   ISBN-13: 978-0-531-17480-7
   ISBN-10: 0-531-17480-8
   1. Peafowl—Growth—Juvenile literature. 2. Peafowl—Development—
   Juvenile literature. I. Title. II. Series.
   QL696.G27M365 2007
   598.6'258—dc22   2006023795

1 2 3 4 5 6 7 8 9 10 R 16 15 14 13 12 11 10 09 08 07

CONTENTS

WORD HUNT

Look for these words as you read. They will be in **bold**.

crest
(krest)

hatch
(hach)

peachick
(**pee**-chik)

egg tooth
(eg tooth)

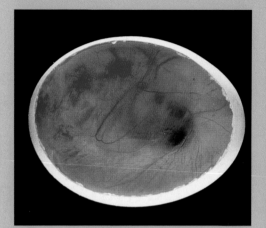

embryo
(**em**-bree-oh)

peacock
(**pee**-kok)

peahen
(**pee**-hen)

5

Peachicks!

Do you see those beautiful feathers? A male peafowl, called a **peacock**, is walking by. Did you know that he was once a plain, brown **peachick**?

How do peachicks grow?

peachick

Peacocks have long, brightly colored feathers.

A female peafowl is called a **peahen**. A peahen usually lays three to eight eggs at a time.

She scratches out a shallow hole in the ground. She uses this hole as a nest for her eggs. The nest is often hidden in tall grass.

A peahen's dull colors help keep her hidden when nesting.

A peahen, like many other birds, keeps her eggs warm by sitting on them.

Each egg contains a developing baby called an **embryo**.

It takes twenty-eight days for an embryo to grow into a peachick.

embryo

Peafowl eggs are light tan.

Finally, the peachicks are ready to **hatch**!

They break out of the eggshells using a special tooth called an **egg tooth**.

A newborn peachick is covered with soft, fuzzy down, or feathers.

egg tooth

This newborn peachick is tired. It can take a peachick several hours to peck out of its shell.

After hatching, a peachick follows its mother around. Peachicks can feed themselves, but the peahen will lead her chicks to food.

Peachicks eat seeds, berries, and insects off of the ground.

They also eat small animals such as snakes!

A peachick stays with its mother for about nine weeks.

Peachicks begin trying to fly about a week after they hatch.

After about four weeks, a peachick grows a **crest** on its head.

As male peachicks get older, their feathers slowly become longer and more colorful.

4 weeks

9 weeks

A peachick's crest grows in over time.

11 weeks

5 months

A peachick becomes an adult peafowl when it is three years old.

Adult males have long, beautiful feathers.

Soon, it will be time for new peachicks to hatch!

Can you tell which adult bird is the peacock and which is the peahen?

A PEACHICK GROWS UP!

1

A peachick embryo takes twenty-eight days to grow.

2

Finally, the baby peachick hatches from its egg!

3

At first, peachicks are soft and fuzzy.

6 A peachick becomes an adult peafowl at three years old.

5 A peachick's feathers grow longer as it gets older. After about four weeks, a crest forms on the peachick's head.

4 Peachicks eat seeds, berries, and insects.

21

YOUR NEW WORDS

crest (krest) a bunch of hair or feathers at the top of an animal's head

egg tooth (eg tooth) a sharp tooth that a hatchling uses to peck open its egg

embryo (**em**-bree-oh) a baby that is growing inside an egg

hatch (hach) to break out of an egg

peachick (**pee**-chik) a baby peafowl

peacock (**pee**-kok) a male peafowl

peahen (**pee**-hen) a female peafowl

THESE ANIMALS ARE BIRDS, TOO!

chicken

ostrich

sparrow

toucan

INDEX

FIND OUT MORE

Book:

Gibson, Kari Smalley, Gary Smalley, and Barbara Spurll (illustrator). *Mooki and the Too-Proud Peacock*. Grand Rapids, MI.: Zonderkidz, 2002.

Website:

Pueblo Zoo Peacock
http://www.pueblozoo.org/archives/mar00/feature.html

MEET THE AUTHOR

Katie Marsico lives with her family outside of Chicago, Illinois. She doesn't own a peacock, but she has a variety of other animals at home, including dogs, fish, and a guinea pig.